W w

Walter in the Woods and the Letter **W**

Alphabet Friends

by Cynthia Klingel and Robert B. Noyed

The Child's World®

Published in the United States of America by The Child's World®
P.O. Box 326
Chanhassen, MN 55317-0326
800-599-READ
www.childsworld.com

The Child's World®: Mary Berendes, Publishing Director

Editorial Directions, Inc.: E. Russell Primm, Editorial Director; Emily Dolbear, Line Editor; Ruth Martin, Editorial Assistant; Linda S. Koutris, Photo Researcher and Selector

Photographs ©: Thinkstock: Cover & 21; Corbis: 9, 13, 17; Michael Boys/Corbis: 10; Image 100/Punchstock: 14; Gary Meszaros/ Dembinsky Photo Associates: 18.

Library of Congress Cataloging-in-Publication Data
Klingel, Cynthia Fitterer.
  Walter in the woods and the letter W / by Cynthia Klingel and Robert B. Noyed.
    p. cm. — (Alphabet readers)
Summary: A simple story about a boy named Walter and how he spent his day exploring the woods introduces the letter "w".
  ISBN 1-59296-113-4 (Library Bound : alk. paper)
  [1. Forests and forestry—Fiction. 2. Alphabet.] I.
Noyed, Robert B., ill. II. Title. III. Series.
  PZ7.K6798Wal 2003
  [E]—dc21   2003006615

Note to parents and educators:
The first skill children acquire before becoming successful readers is individual letter recognition. The Alphabet Friends series has been created with the needs of young learners in mind. Each engaging book begins by showing the difference between the capital letter and the lowercase letter. In each of the books on the vowels and the consonants c and g, children are introduced to the different sounds that the letter can make. Finally, children see that the letters can be found at the beginning of a word, in the middle of a word, and in most cases, at the end of a word.

Following the introduction, children meet their Alphabet Friends. The friend in each story encounters many words that include the featured letter of that book. Each noun that begins with the title letter is highlighted in red with the initial letter of the word in bold. Above the word is a rebus drawing that establishes a strong picture cue.

At the end of each book, we have included three words lists. Can your young learners find all the words in each book with the title letter in them?

Let's learn about the letter **W.**

The letter **W** can look like this: **W.**

The letter **W** can also look like this: **w.**

The letter **w** can be at the

beginning of a word, like woods.

woods

The letter **w** can be in the

middle of a word, like newspaper.

ne**w**spaper

The letter **w** can be at the end of a word, like rainbow.

rainbo**w**

Walter watched the birds fly overhead.

Their **w**ings were spread wide. **W**alter

watched them dive and soar in the **w**ind.

Walter and his dad had the whole day

to wander in the **w**oods. He walked

down the wide path. **W**ildflowers grew

along the path.

Walter saw the **w**ater at the edge of the

woods. He was hot. The **w**ater would feel

good. He jumped in.

Waves spread out around him. Walter

wiggled his toes in the water. He could

see fish swim around his legs.

A big fish swam close by. It was a

walleye! **W**alter was excited to see the

walleye. He swam after the fish.

Walter waded out of the **w**ater.

The **w**ind was getting wild. **W**alter

wondered if it would storm.

It was time to walk home. **W**alter and

his dad had spent a wonderful afternoon

in the **w**oods. He would wait and do it

another day.

Fun Facts

 The walleye is a kind of fish in the perch family. It lives in large rivers and lakes in North America. Walleyes eat other fish and an animal called the crayfish. A walleye can grow to be as long as 36 inches (91 centimeters)—that's 3 feet long! The walleye is a popular sport fish, which means fishers like to catch walleyes. The fish also makes a tasty meal.

 What do bats, birds, and insects all have in common? They all have wings! Wings help many of these animals to fly, but are useful in other ways as well. For example, wings help water birds—like ducks—to dive and swim. Other birds, such as the turkey, use their wings as weapons. Some animals use their wings to express emotion or to communicate. When a male cricket is looking for a mate, for instance, he rubs his front wings together to produce a courtship song.

To Read More

About the Letter W
Flanagan, Alice K. *Wish and Win: The Sound of W.* Chanhassen, Minn.: The Child's World, 2000.

About Walleye
Angelfish, Christopher, and Joe Veno (illustrator). *The Fish Book.* Racine, Wis.: Golden Books Publishing, 1997.

Cohen, Caron Lee, S.D. Schindler (pictures). *How Many Fish?* New York: HarperCollinsPublishers, 1998.

Pfister, Marcus, and J. Alison James (translator). *Rainbow Fish.* New York: North-South Books, 1992.

About Wings
Ehlert, Lois. *Waiting for Wings.* San Diego: Harcourt, 2001.

Taravant, Jacques, and Nina Ignatowicz (translator), and Peter Sis (illustrator). *The Little Wing Giver.* New York: Henry Holt, 2001.

Words with W

Words with W at the Beginning

waded
wait
walk
walked
walleye
Walter
wander
was
watched
water
waves
were
whole
wide
wiggled
wild
wildflowers
wind
wings
wondered
wonderful
woods
word
would

Words with W in the Middle

down
newspaper
swam
swim

Words with W at the End

grew
rainbow
saw

About the Authors

Cynthia Klingel has worked as a high school English teacher and an elementary teacher. She is currently the curriculum director for a Minnesota school district. Cynthia Klingel lives with her family in Mankato, Minnesota.

Robert B. Noyed started his career as a newspaper reporter. Since then, he has worked in communications and public relations for a Minnesota school district for more than fourteen years. Robert B. Noyed lives with his family in Brooklyn Center, Minnesota.